The Stickman Chronicles

PERPLEXED

by Keith J. Doucet

Dorrance Publishing Co
585 Alpha Drive
Pittsburgh, PA 15238
Visit our website at *www.dorrancebookstore.com*

ISBN: 978-1-6480-4634-6
eISBN: 978-1-6480-4650-6

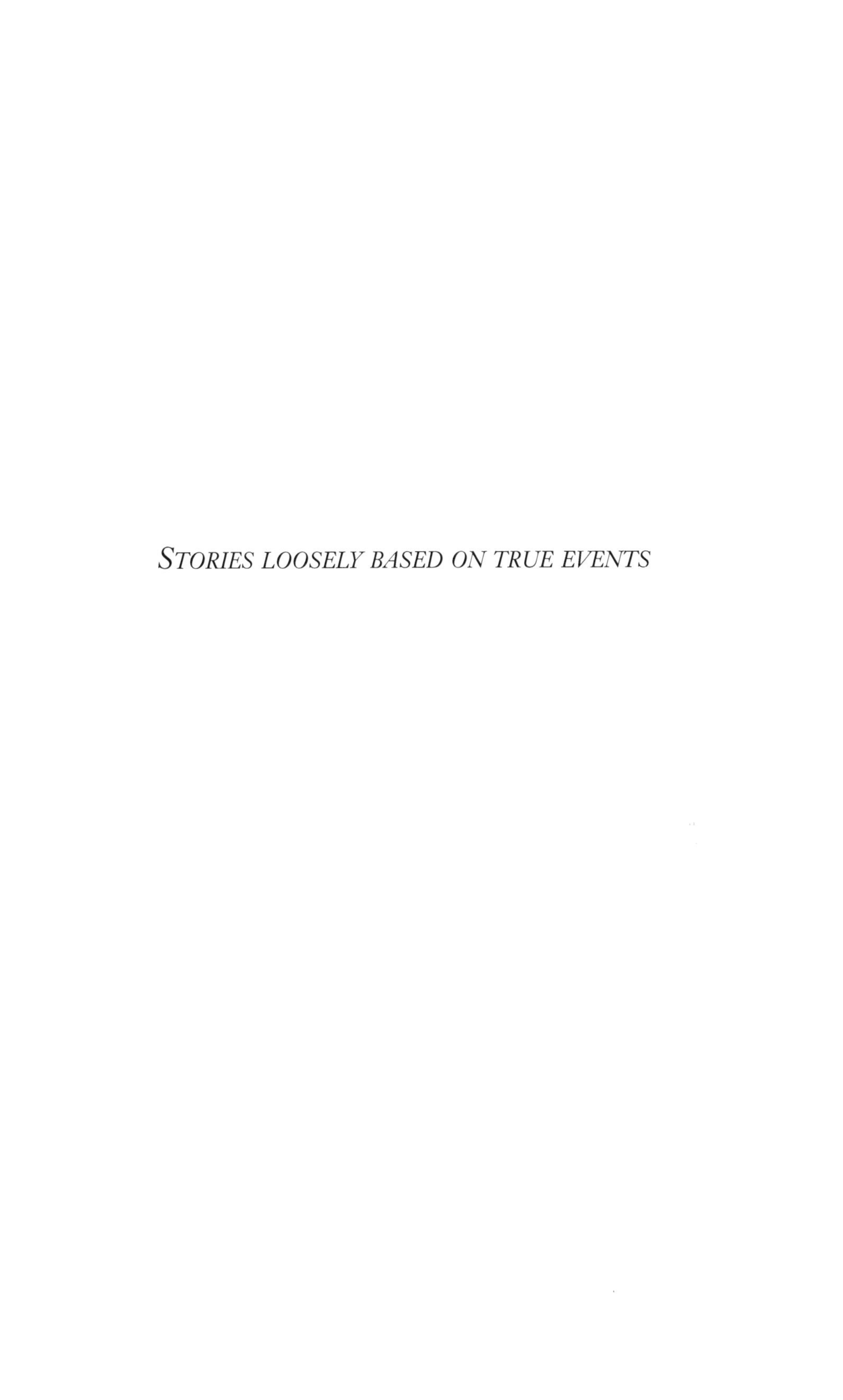

Stories loosely based on true events

CHAPTER 1
Thanks

Be to the Lord, always and forever, I spend most days perplexed by my future and my possibilities, only the love of the Lord and my son KEATON get me through the days and hours. I really don't know what is going on in my mind; every moment feels like a déjà vu. It freaks me out sometimes. I mean, is it my mind, or am I able to predict the future? I can't continue letting people and things trigger my skittish state of being; some people think it's funny and a joke, but in reality, it sometimes wants to just end my life, but my faith pulls me through. Not to mention the pain and memory of watching my baby brother whom I loved as if he were my own child die in my arms, murdered by his close childhood friend. So sad, so sad and disturbing.

I have enough misery in my life, yet people want to test me, or is it me testing my own existence? Did I cause this skittish behavior; did I chose to be alone?

On this day, September 16, 2015, I no longer will be moved by my so-called friends, my selfish friends. I will not budge. It seems like everyone is in a chaotic dimension, and I'm rejecting its offer to join and partake in its wild illusions of reality; maybe I should experiment, but something is holding me back. It seems obvious to the humans in its twist and turns, and my direction has description, the path of free will. I rely on the only thing that gives me comfort, and that is Jesus; he is my strength, and he is not my secret. He can be the savior for all and anyone who believes, so I'm just gonna let him lead, and I trust that my sufferings in the past will diminish and wither away so I can enjoy my life here with my son and family. And even my selfish friends, my life is good only because that the things I aquired are a sign from the Lord giving me a taste of my treasures which I have built up in heaven. They are only material, but I believe the Lord is just making me comfortable and rewards the humble, and I have truly become humble and appreciate even the smallest possessions. Well, in my suffering for me and my family and friends. I truly love and pray for all of you and myself; I hope they do the same. GOD bless.

Sept. 17, 2015

Another day of weirdness and paranoia ,but I reflect back and see an alter ego that I created as a child.

I never was comfortable in a social setting, including school, and even family, so I became Kebee, a twisted sense of humor and intimidation at its best peak of fear. I would pour out to society; now I am nowhere close to that guy, just stories of Kebee's life and times, some legendary. Oh, what a past it was, but it is past; now it's a humble life, and I'm okay with that but do wish I had a woman in my life to love and to love back. GOD BLESS.

Sept 19, 2015

Loving my time with Keaton; he makes everything better. GOD BLESS.

Man, some people are hard to reach, but I know they can be reached. I'm trying to save my friend's soul or punishment for his denial of Jesus. I'm making sense by using my way of reaching the misinformed using scripture and the message of the Lord and savior. He is very clever and smart. Also, it's my battle; I'll win. It's making me stronger in faith. Wow, what a challenge.

My wretched ass will prove through the holy spirit and his word; I'll keep on.

Sept 24

I don't write every day, because not a whole lot of anything going on. I'm trying to work up the energy to write my memoires, but it's difficult to put in words because I can't remember most of the legendry moments, and now my beliefs and my relentless study of the Bible, mostly my interest in Paul, who wrote most of the new testament. I really relate to his letters to the churches and their people, but back to my past; wow, man, what a ride. I'm sure there are some aphorisms out there due to my encounters and storytelling with a point of knowledge and self-proclaimed wisdom of an outlaw. Hey, I think I just wrote the name of my book, *Wisdom of an Outlaw*, lol.

October 4, 2015

I am truly perplexed in my thinking and lazy on writing. I know I got good material but don't know if I even want to stir up all these memories of the legendary past. I get reminded of people I really would like to do harm to. I need a trip with some peace and tranquility away from home. At least my favorite person in this crazy world is with me. Thank you, Jesus for Keaton. It's ironic that there is no woman in my life at the moment. I always was lucky with beautiful women, natural charm. It was easy for me to just walk in a place and pick up the hottest chick there, and I was hated by many for this gift, so I hear, haters, huh? I also was a hustler in the drug game and was good at that also, lol. Hard dope, fast women, lots of cash, but there comes a time when you know you pushed the limits and get out before you get killed by a new, young version of who I thought I was to be. Hey, let's be logical. I couldn't continue that forever. I had to move aside for the new kid on the block, so I gracefully stepped down, which my motivation stirred up from learning that I was gonna be a father, and that's where the transition begins, man. The last few hours been playing guitar and got some pretty good tunes. I still am a harmonica player first, but I'm down depressed Keaton gone. I'm alone again. About to be my birthday; "so fucking what?" I'm more depressed. I can't make myself tell these fucking stories, scared it will be as if I'm glorifying the horrible fucking pain and chaos in this town I unleashed with criminals worse than me. What a wretch I am; I don't deserve to tell these particular times and crimes against humanity, man. Fucking, I am a bad seed that somehow grew into a fucking jungle, man. "I'm not worthy."

October 11

My birthday came and went, nothing special, hung out with Keaton a couple days out the week. That's my everything, but now my mind is in chaos again. At times, I'm delusional, but I keep them to myself. I'm paranoid of everyone; it's fucking miserable, but that's how it goes for me. I'm broken, and I have faith things will become clear once again, so I'm kinda down these days. I did everything wrong and still somehow maintaining, but no one really knows how close to a complete breakdown I'm fighting and fighting. So fricking lonely but too crazy to be around anyone. I'm praying for forgiveness because this is a direct effect of the past lifestyle I lived through. Maybe, one day, I can tell these stories. I'm working the courage up. Lord, give me peace, show me mercy; I suffered long enough, but I guess you will make that call. God bless.

October 15, 2015

Well, my mental state has been randomly switching to sane to insane, but I'm really in to playing music. I am advancing in my guitar playing; that has been keeping me from just being idle, and the rest of my days is studying the scripture. My love life only exists in my memories of my missed opportunity of what I believe was my true love Katy, but I understand that she will always be in my heart and mind. She is gone, and I dont think she is coming back. It's been ten years. I'll never forget how I fell in love with her. I was leaving her house and was thinking the fine ass woman will never want to be with a guy like me, so I announced that I was leaving. She was laying in the bed because we were hanging in her room after partying for a couple days with my true friend Chad, which who is responsible for bringing me there.

Well, as I'm walking past her, she looks up at me and grabs my hand, and I'm staring down at this beautiful angel, and she says to me, "Don't leave me; don't ever leave me," and in that instance, I knew we were in love, and I bent down and kissed her, because one thing that I believe is the most passionate is a kiss. I'll never forget how she looked at me, and we had many more fantastic moments that I will soon write about, including my true friend Chad, but back to the present time. I know where my happiness and peace lives; it's with my best friend Nevaeh. She brings joy to my inner being; just being in her presence lights me up. She makes me feel more like myself than ever, so I have found my happiness and peace with Nevaeh and found my love that lives with Katy, and I'm speaking of a essence of these emotions that feed me with these two beauties. I seem to understand this, but it is perplexing. Physically, I can't have either one, for reasons that only they could give that answer to. Why would they not be with me? Other than as my spiritual roommates, sort of speak.

She doesn't see that way; she is special to me. She has a gift, a pleasure to be in her presence. I'm lucky to have had these two women in my life. Only God knows if I'll ever have a future wife to spend life with me and my everything, my son Keaton. The story of Keaton's life of how that came to be is truly the work of God. I knew that there was gonna be a pregnancy by either Heather or Katy because I slept with both of them just days apart. I'm not bragging about that. Just at that time I had made a decision that I loved Katy, and it was over with Heather, and I left Katy's house to go finalize the end of me and Heather. Well, we agreed, Heather and I, but I was getting high on meth as we discussed just being friends. Well, somehow, we had sex. I know it was wrong, but it happened. Well, I was gone for two days without realizing that much time passed by; meth can do that to you. Time seems to disappear. Well, by the time I got back to Katy's, she met me on the porch as I pulled up on my motorcycle and told me, "I'm marrying my ex." I'm like, fuck, how long have I been gone? This broke my heart, truly. Now it's over with Heather, and now it's over with Katy. Well, anyway, I knew that God told me a child was coming. I was right; a month later Heather tells me she is pregnant. It's how God wanted it, so I lost two women but got the greatest gift God could give, and to me, that is Keaton, but I'm gettin' ahead of the times of Kebee. I'll continue on a later date. God bless.

BACK TO THE YEAR OF 2005

Okay, I'm gonna tell these experiences in humbling sort of speak. I mentioned earlier about some stories I would talk about so, let's call this volume one of a series that will come in another book, titled *The Stickman Chronicles*. Here we go. I found myself broke and confused in Jackson, Mississippi, in bad weather when I picked up a hitchhiker, mostly hoping he had money for gas. Unfortunately, no, he did not but promised he could get money. My thoughts were I could just leave him standing roadside in the rain; what kind of person would do that? Well not me. He was so relieved someone had stopped for him. His name was Arthur. Never will I forget him and our journey together for a few hours. Well, I'm in bad shape due to the partying I have done over the past few days prior, so Arthur asked me, "What the hell is wrong with you, son?" So, hey, I know he is not the police. He was a medium-built guy about my size, sort of average. He was not particularly scary looking at all. He had a good aura about him, a lil' dirty from being on the road, I guess.

I was very paranoid in those days, mainly because I was an outlaw in the means of drug dealer/womanizer; well, one of them is illegal. "Well, Arthur," I responded, "you see, I met this girl in my hometown, Lafayette, Louisiana,. from my ecstasy supplier on Christmas Eve. She's a cousin of my supplier, and we hit off, and she asked if I would take her back to Mississippi, if she stayed an extra day, which was cause to lose her ride if she stayed. Of course, I agreed; what else did I have to do? Plus, she was stunning and a great kisser. I'm a sucker for that. Her name was Cody; a boy's name was even sexier to me. I don't like boys, just like girls with boys' names, so me and Cody take off the day after Christmas on a cocaine vein injecting binge, stopping all along the way to rig up another fix. It took eight hours for a four-hour trip, so we get to Cody's apartment, and her roommate, which I for the likes of me cannot remember her name; well, anyway, she sells us some acid. Within the first moments of entering the apartment, man, I knew better than to do that shit, on the account that two days before I met Cody I just returned from a regular weed run in Houston and partied with a childhood friend, Christine, who also was my connection. It was an abundance of many substances, so I haven't slept in a week by now, and I kept getting confused of my surroundings, geographically speaking, not to mention Cody's apartment was similar to Christine's in Houston. So, finally at its peak of the acid trip, on top of everything else, sleep deprivation and all, I managed to clumsily have sex with Cody, and everything from there is cloudy because I fell out then, only to wake up talking on the phone to who I thought was an old friend. As, I conversed with my old friend, whom I thought it to be on the line and giving him directions to where I was at and told him these chicks have access to many different narcotics, then suddenly I hear Cody screaming "Get off the phone!" and I was alerted and alarmed to hear that I was speaking with Cody's mother in my drug-induced coma. I answered her phone and was talking out the side of my neck. Well, Cody commenced in telling me, after she assured her mother that I was just joking around and she was absolutely safe, and that I had gotten up and pissed in the closet, then began rambling on and on about how in reality we are just Barbie and Ken dolls. I have no recollection of these strange moments she is describing. After hearing all this, I asked, "How long have I been asleep?" She responds, "About seven hours."

"Oh," I say, thinking "not enough." Then she breaks the news to me: "You need to leave." It seems she really did not feel safe at all. So, I get dressed, check my belongings, including my funds; boom, I'm fucking broke. She claims I spent my money, but damn, all of it? That's out of character, but who knows? I was in a twisted binge and all I could do was leave because now I'm afraid she is so afraid of me that she would call the police. Well, I asked, "May I please take a shower?" She AGREED and left me to do just that, and that's when I saw the canvas, blank, bright white canvas on an easel. Blank, I fucking tell you.

I was so tempted I could not refrain myself, so I drew a fucking plain-Jane stick man with black paint next to the easel.

There the stickman was born. To this day, I would love to see her reaction after seeing that; who does that kind of shit? I asked Arthur. His words were "Fucking Kebee, man. Fucking Kebee, man." I'm liking this Arthur guy, especially after he directs me to a truck stop and tells me wait for him, and I did. I couldn't go anywhere as I say to him, "We running on fumes,." Twenty minutes later, he comes back with thirty-four dollars that he panhandled and even a half pack of smokes. All right, Arthur.

So, here we go again, on the road, Kebee and Arthur cruising with a full tank of gas in a lil' green Ford Ranger. Now comes the part of Arthur's wisdom. He gave me the keys to some powerful knowledge and insight of the universe and all that is in it.

Sadly, to your disappointment, he had me promise not to repeat or share with anyone but utilize it in actions and not in words, so as the man I am, I will honor that and still do this day, which he made this man become a little child that burst into a heartbroken cry, lip trembling, snorting from the nose cry. Then I asked the question that I should have asked the moment he got in the truck, “Where you headed, Arthur?”

“Arizona, Kebee,” he said, then he was crying now.

“Hey,” I said, “hey, man, what is it?”

“I’m going home to see my momma.” He was really crying it up. He continued saying, “Haven’t seen her in many years, Kebee, because I lived the life you living now.” That’s all he had to say. I understood what he meant. He needed to say no more. Louisiana state line, baby. I’m almost home. Then Arthur asked, “Hey, come with me, me and you, Kebee and Arthur.”

I said, after a minute or so of really thinking hard, very hard, then, I, like him, loved my momma, and I couldn’t leave my momma, and he smiled and said, “That’s right, son.” We get to Lafayette; I pull into a gas station, said our goodbyes, and I gave him all my clothes that I brought along for the trip, even clean socks and underwear, and that was that. I still wonder if he made it to his momma. I want to believe he did.

CHAPTER 2

Dope in the Attic

I get home, sleep for almost two days, and a knock on the door, not sure what day it is, hoping didn't miss the New Year's parties and hoping it's not the police, but I know their knock is a lot stronger and louder than this sort of a soft, don't want to disturb knock. I look through the peep hole, and it Christine with a smile, and I was glad to see her here in Lafayette because that meant that I didn't have to go back to Houston. I let her in, and she gave me the normal hug as always. I love that. Well, she starts explaining that she made the run by herself, and she has a duffle bag with 5 lbs. of weed in it, and in asking, "Why just five?", and then she explains the other five which would complete the order of 10 lbs. is at a safe house in the basin for a very good reason. If you gonna ride dirty, then keep half somewhere, for if the police stop you and find it, they only get half, and the half is insurance, sort of speak, it's money, well, bail money, and you or someone else brings the other half or you go back and get it yourself. Hard to find loyalty these days. So, the apartment complex I live in just so happens that my townhome has the attic access to the four other adjoining townhomes, so I jump on the stair banister and climb up in the attic, and Christine hands me the weed, and I crawl down about three apartments down from mine and stash it under a roll of insulation. It is also where I stash a couple of firearms that I dabble in the sales of to people that can't get because of many reasons, like mentally unstable or a felon, that are unable to purchase firearms with the background check that applies. So, I climb down slide the cover back, and I shower.

Getting dressed in my normal attire, which is usually blue jeans and a T-shirt and always cowboy boots, always. I'll explain my love of cowboy boots later. I run my fingers through my hair. I haven't brushed my hair since 1989, and I, at the time, had long black hair and kept my face clean shavened, so I run down stairs, and Christine asks to go ride on the night train a 2002 Harley that sleeps in the dining room of my townhouse, but it was kinda chilly out, and I needed to get the other 5 lbs. back here because the drop off was to be before New Year's Eve which now was in two days, and I promised Heather I would bring in the New Year with her. This is where Heather comes into the story which will ultimately change our lives forever and bond us together for the rest of our lives, and I still need to get with Chad and my little brother Randy who live in the same complex. Me and Chad had plans to go to an open mic night downtown to a blues and jazz club where a friend, Cotton Gin Tim, has a share in the club. Tim actually lives in an old cotton gin, over a hundred years old, that was converted into a cool fucking house surrounded by nine acres of land and bamboo all over the property, totally secluded. Wow, the fucking times over there is another whole story in The Stickman Chronicles, but before I do anything, I have to score some motivation, which comes through my love and addiction to crystal meth, so that first, then meet Chad and Randy for what I've really been excited for a couple weeks. We were getting paid for a little. Well, I'm sorry; I can't give details of what went on to gain a small fortune for us that would support us for at least the next year, but back to present time. I will get back to story soon.

October 18, 2015

Remembering and putting the past of my life and times down in writing, bittersweet, bittersweet.

All I can say is I got a few things I have to leave out due to could cause problems legally and, most of all, physically by people that live by certain laws and rules that they enforce and written by the old way that goes back generations, but these days, I stay to myself and raise my son along with Heather but separately. Me and her have a good system and agreement that works phenomenally. I'm struggling these days still. I mean, mentally. It's a curse that GOD has stuck down on me due to my past. I'm forgiven by him because I asked and pleaded for it and begged for mercy. So, it is what it is, as my best friend Nevaeh would say. I hope to see her soon; I need her in my life, and she hasn't been around lately, but I know it will be not too much longer. I pray and I pray for her and her son that they are safe and favored by the good Lord. I include them in my constant prayers for Keaton, my family, and Chad and a few others. Never do I forget to praise and thank him for what I have. I do not feel worthy at times, but I know, and he knows, my heart, and I owe everything to Jesus. I love him and only made it through this world up till today because of him. I'm telling this story, *The Stickman Chronicles: Volume One*, which means I'm only writing about a week or two of endeavors, and I hope to write more about future endeavors.

GOD bless.

Well, can't sleep, so I'm gonna continue with today's writing. I want people to know that some things I will be writing I'm not proud of, and I'm sure one day my parents and even my son will read these things I put down about my past, and all I can say is there is no future in the past. I'm not that man anymore. I am single, mental, including OCD with intrusive thoughts.

My life is very frustrating and difficult, only because of the hard past. I don't want to seem in any way that I'm glorifying my past, because most people will not make it out like I did, and trust there is some funny shit that I encountered here and there in my journeys, along with some interesting characters that you will think that it could not be true, but this no tall tale. These things, these little moments burnt in my mind, well, what's left of it, with exception to having to change some names, times, and locations. All on account of be investigated by local and government authorities.

UNKNOWN DATE

I know, I know that I know! I'm on the right road, but I'm going the wrong fucking direction.

CHAPTER 3
GETTING PAID

Just scored an eight-ball of meth that will do just fine, on the count of I get nothing but the best shit in town, so that's all a person needs and even enough to share with Chad. Now I'm back in the complex to meet Chad. Chad is a good, honest guy. I mean, he even looks honest. He is a stocking guy with never a bad word or a bad attitude toward anyone. I mean it, man. He is a good guy. I never seen him lose his temper, which worries me, because I'm afraid for the one that gets it if he ever decides to unleash all that fury built up. So, he greets me at the door with a smile and "what's up?" Well, what's up is where is the cash? He explains that Randy is holding it and waiting for us. So, we start to walk over toward Randy's apartment right down a few rows from Chad. Now, my lil' brother, who is ten years younger than I, is a tall, fit young man with eyes that memorize women, along with a smile of innocence plus a little bit of bad boy in his aura. He can really make me laugh, and man, I tell you, I need a good laugh often. So, Randy greets us at the door. His girl, Lexi is cleaning up is, what it looks like, after their son Ashton. I'm ready to roll a bowl of dope, but Randy grabs his backpack and says, "Hey, let's go to Chad's." Okay, so back to Chad's. There we roll the dice, and I'm high now. Let's get to it. We split the cash and ramble on about really nothing because I'm not really listening anyway. I'm nodding yes to everything with an occasional yeah, yeah, but Chad gets my attention when he brings up the story about a fine-ass, cool chick he met at the store and then followed her to her house to get high and party. He goes on and on of how cool this chick was and insisting that I meet her. Now, understand, I have never had problems with meeting women none ever, ever, and Chad wants to bring me to meet this one, knowing how most women draw to my energy and charm that I can't stop. It's a gift.

I know I sound arrogant, but I'm just repeating what others say about me when it comes to women. Anyway, I agreed to check her out.

Boy, I wasn't prepared for what would eventually come to be a revelation who I would later come to be, but before we make plans to hook up with this girl named Katy, I need to get the 5 lbs. from the house in the basin. Two days till New Year's Eve and all of us are feeling great. We decide to stick together, because we feed off one another. Randy suggests taking the bikes. He rode a '93 FXR Harley, and Chad was a Honda man, which I respect, and to me, two wheels is two wheels as I would ride with Chad anywhere. I'm resisting saying its "kinda chilly," and I get a response of "pussy." That's all it took, and I'm walking to get my bike from in my apartment, and we plan to meet in a half hour so Randy could convince Lexi to go with us. I knew she would, because like me, my little bro has a way of persuasion and always makes a point of making the person of the persuasion feel like they have to agree with us. It's another gift.

PRESENT TIME - OCTOBER 20, 2015

Not much happening with me, the usual boredom, day after day, but man, I have to say, "Bored over the dramas that paved my past."

Like, shit, can't think of a metaphor or an aphorism at this moment. Funny how I can just be blank-minded when I think about those days and how sure I was of myself and anyone along with me that we were unstoppable in our endeavors. Today it scares the living fuck right out of me. We were some lucky sons of bitches. I'm still feeling the repercussions of the stickman. I'm a thankful man every day! I want to cry, but the Dr. got me on Prozac for OCD and depression, so the ability to cry tears is dried up, but the sadness in my heart penetrates deep through and through, where you can see it by the look on my face. My eyes seem dead as if no life .Pitiful days are frequent. I hang on waiting with being in love with waiting. God bless.

October 21, 2015

Man, its 2 A.M. Hey, what the fuck does A.M. mean anyway? Why don't I know that? Let me tell you, I can't sleep. I need to let everyone know about me and Chad. I met him in the year of 1988 or 1989. Through the years, we have gotten closer, as time slips pass us like a north wind in January, cuttin' through us and peeling off the young man face to a cold and bitter face that we never stopped to notice because we were young and paving the way to legendary. Chad is a highly intelligent man, an artist of paintings, music, and sculptures. He is very creative and can converse with anyone in any situation. He has an innocent look and a kind voice. So, I'm tossing and turning last night thinking about my longtime friend. It hits me after all these years; "What the fuck is he doing hanging around me?" No, I'm not that bad, but I definitely have learned more from him, and he has talked me out of a lot of life changing moments for the benefit of lots of people at times. I would believe that he has learned a lil' from my chaos. He stimulates the intellect in me. We have conversed for days at a time and are never bored with each other. We are always searching to learn something we had not known before, important things, history, the Bible, magic, the universe. Our conversations always begins in a... hey, did you know this?

Ante meridum? Now I know what A.M. stands for. I wonder if anyone else didn't know. Fucking ringing in my ear is constant. it is driving me crazy, "crazier."

I often sit here and wonder. I mean, it seems to me that a lot of people I called friends abandoned me, or did I abandon them? I guess due the fact I lost all control of logic in my thinking, and I haven't really gained my full sanity back. You wouldn't know because I hide it well. There are people that don't understand me any longer, so I've been in solitude for about nine years, maybe ten. Chad is the only one besides my family that is patient and understanding of my horror. My little sister, Angie, oh, how do I ever thank her? For her being the best sister I could ever ask for. I'm particularly proud of the woman she has become after growing up with three brothers, with Randy, her twin, me ten years older, and Mike, two years older than me. I could have been a better role model. I always thought of myself as a leader, but never said I was a good one. I dragged a lot of good people down the road to nowhere; that road leads back to me.

Now, let tell you this, "Average is the worst of best and the best of worst," and I refused to be average in those days. Today I run in to old girlfriends and childhood friends and they have accomplished their dreams, as it seems to others, nice homes, great jobs, two children, swimming pools, golf on Sunday afternoons, block parties, real white people, you dig. When I run across these suburban mutants, I greet them with a smile, and I am, I really am, deep down, am envious and think I could be living in the same manner. Now, at the same moment, these mutants of the grand society are somehow also envious of my life and would love to live it, but it would be only as transient guest. I'm sure of this. a wish it was temporary for me as well, too late to ever completely remove the mission of the stickman. It was not as bad as it seems, you know, playing music downtown in the bars. I once played harmonica, which is kinda an attribute of Kebee. I love blowing some blues out the harps, like I'm making the wind cry. I played at a well-known club on Mardi Grad day; that was a great performance, and me and Chad were frequently on the scene. Sometimes, writing a song as we wait for our time to play. Need not to say that it was definitely a plus in picking women up. Once a guy says to me, "Kebee, you only get pussy because you got a bike and the dope." I reply, "Well, then you should get a bike and sell dope." I mean it didn't hurt those things, but I didn't need that to score a piece of ass. At one bar one evening I'm relaxing in a bar that I didn't frequent, and the bar maid was hot, so I make small talk that I could see the guy on the other side of the bar that probably been there all day or even every day for the last week trying to get that ass, all along spending his whole check running up his credit card and tipping her; that's her fucking job, idiot. This is what I'm thinking by the way he is looking at me. Fuck him. I turn it on buying her a shot to shoot with me and keep her entertained by running some Kebeeism on her. Okay, let me explain. The hardest women to pick up is the bar maid. Think about it. She hears every pick-up line ever, she is in constant restraint of wanting to scream out, "Leave me alone and just order a drink," damn hard legs, so I give props to the ones that, at the end of her shift, she agrees to leave with you. Now, after about thirty minutes of me make her blush and giggle, the hard leg runs up on me, and he was quick. I barely made up off the stool to defend myself, and boom, he spits these words out his alcoholic fumed mouth, "You slick, slimey, silver-tongue speaking son of a bitch." I simply agreed with him and left, with the bartender, ha, ha. Those days can just pile up on a person like myself. What a weird thing (the past).

Before you patronize me like I'm used to, let me peel back the suit of ugliness and remind everyone about why I'm writing *The Stickman Chronicles*, simply to explain how Keaton came into my life. GOD himself, the strategist that he is, knew that I was not going to be in this world much longer, and I was expecting to retire from the suffering I put on myself. Suicide is not my style, although in the reality of it, I was attempting to kill myself daily, hourly, with the excessive and abundance of drugs and alcohol and women on a motorbike through most of these times. The reason I believe I had to numb myself constantly is purely that I am introvert seeking solace in disguise as an extrovert, while I apply my introspection of myself and anyone that I make contact with. Yes, the irony harnessed by me, "the hyper vigilant," along with a structural theory and opinion of the depths of our existence. But hey, I'm just a rube with an eighth-grade education. What in the hell do I have to give back to the world? I'm a nobody that everybody wants to be around me. At this point of my invasion of the streets of Lafayette has expected to die at any time. Then everything just came to a screeching halt. That alone sent me to do some vacationing in a mental hospital on two occasions. My mental state was diagnosed as if I returned from war, suffering from PTSD and needed to be debriefed. Thank you, Lord, for my son, my gift, my reckoning that cleared the view. So, back to the story.

CHAPTER 4
W.F.O.

Before I get my bike out the house, I stash my cash, except for five hundred dollars for pocket money, my stash place for the remainder of my bulk of cash simply in a Tupperware in the back of my freezer behind, I'm pretty sure, some outdated frozen food. Then I draw a nice line of meth, roll up a crisp hundred-dollar bill to snort it up my nose. Man, that shit burns. Why do I like this shit? Now I have about three grams left of the eight-ball I scored earlier.

Eight-ball is three-and-a-half grams, and I smoked with Chad and Randy and snorted a line that's about a half gone .Then my paranoid mind kicks in like a wrecking ball. I'm suddenly rethinking this bike ride on the fact of, first thing, I hide two grams of meth, because I don't need to travel with that much anyway; a gram was plenty of this shit. I talk myself into a calm and imagined me lying in a green pasture with the sun gently breathing its warmth upon my cold flesh, only to be interrupted by the sound of knocking on the door. I jump up, check my nose in the mirror, quietly creep up to the peephole, and what I see is beautiful to me. Now, the thing is, I do not recognize this young lady. I run my hands through my hair real quick and open the door with a, "Can I help you?" Then, with a lil' smirk and giggle, "Please tell me, can I help you?" Now, what happens in the next moments will seem unbelievable. this is where my witnesses will come into play to verify the truth of it. That was because of some quick thinking to have witnesses to this great moment in *The Stickman Chronicles*. Well, a great moment for me anyway. I'll never forget this strange encounter that I can't believe it myself. I've been lucky, but this is overboard lucky. "Hi, my name is ???" Now, get this, I can't remember her fucking name, really I can't, and I never seen or heard from her again to this day. Okay, I say, "Can I help you?" as I'm moving side to side and speaking very fast and almost as if it was I'm speaking in another language, starting to tweek a lil', feeling pretty damn good. I feel like I'm the most important person I know. Ha, ha. Meth tends to make you think you are better looking than you really are and that all eyes are on you. You kinda become your dream alter-ego and display it in an odd manner and twitching robotic movements with sound effects from a bad seventies' porn flick echoing under your breath but completely audible. "You sure can." This incredible hot chick with a body straight out of a model swimsuit magazine beautiful is how I refer to her when I talk about our encounter. Man, her eyes were so beautiful that there is no name for the color. They were just mesmerizing, like cat eyes, three different colors it seemed, furthest from the pupil was green then bluish grey, then closest to the pupil was a light brown. Now she begins to tell me that she has been seeing me around different bars and she been too shy to approach me because I'm always with a few different people. That sounds right to me. She goes on of how a mutual friend, she never told me who, really didn't care that someone had given her the location of where I'm living, which was no secret. So, I invite her in, and she grabs me and starts kissing me. You know I'm a sucker for kissing. I start to slow it down and act. Yes, I act like I'm all cool, but I'm intimidated by her looks. She was the most beautiful girl I believe has ever shown interested in me physically. Beauty, I'm describing. I offer her a bump of ish; she accepts the offer then asks for two.

Now, I been with a good number of women but never a ten on a scale of one to ten, been with five twos but don't think that counts. Anyway, she is an easy ten. Now I'm thinking I need proof of this. Then again she walks up to me and starts kissing me all over. Who is this mystery woman? So I pick up my cell phone, and back then, some phones had a two-way radio. Phones weren't as advanced as today, having a two-way radio conversation with ones compatible to yours was a big deal, so I radio Chad to hurry and come over and saying, ""You have to come see this," but I mistakenly called Randy and continued to tell over the phone that she was giving me oral sex. Randy quickly interrupted me and let me know that he wasn't Chad and that everyone in his house just heard me. Embarrassed? No, not really. I call Chad and made sure I got him this time. A few moments later, Chad shows up, and we calm down our sexual desire for a short period. Chad wasted no time in his agreement that she was gorgeous, then Randy shows up minutes later. He also agrees. Now they are asking when we are hitting the road, And we all do another bump of my stash, and now we are all rambling, telling different stories all at once. I ask them to go ahead without me and would catch up with them a lil' later. They had no problem with that. They understood just as I would if the shoe were on the other foot. So, me and the mystery woman get back down to where we were. I hear Randy and Chad taking off from the main road and, like my mind and I'm sure theirs, they were WIDE FUCKING OPEN. I could still hear the rumble of their bikes for at least a minute, then gradually growing a little more faded as they headed down the highway. My mind is back on this sexy beast. My mind would stay on this concentrating, focusing on pleasing this woman in going the distance and further. This went on for about two hours, so I'm feeling intoxicated by her presence and want to take her along with me.

This does not happen. She tells me she has to go, and I did my best to convince her to stay with me. She was adamant in her having to leave, so I ask for her number as we walk out to her car. She simply hugs me, gives me a kiss on the cheek, and says, "It was great, our time together, Kebee," and gets in her car and drove away, never to be seen or heard from again. I'm perplexed and even paranoid at one moment, thinking she may be a narcotics agent ,but I get logical in my thought process and know they wouldn't go that far under cover, or she really loves her job and would go to as far as we went. No, no way. i come to believe she is most likely married or is shacked up with a guy and needed to release some twisted fantasy she had. That works for me. I had never been used in that way before. I was left with mixed emotions about this wild rendezvous. I know this, and that is I have a date with Heather, who had a place in my heart and made me feel a sense of comfort when I was in her presence. I liked that a lot. I'm not comfortable in or around people and situations unless I'm drunk or buzzed with some kind of narcotic. Finally, I get my bike out and radio Chad and Randy, asking for their twenty (location). I have to admit, I'm feeling pretty fucking great right at this moment. I mean I been with several women but never did one ever come on that strong. Believe it or not, but I don't know how not to wear my heart on my sleeve. I fall in love quickly. I learned how to hide the hurt well. I get hurt often because of my soft heart when it comes to women.

I love women, period! They are beautiful creatures that cannot be understood. Trust me, the answer is not at the bottom of a whiskey bottle.

Boom. Randy calls back; they are at a bar in the neighboring town. I gear up, leather shirt over my T-shirt, leather pants over my long johns, cowboy boots, welder's cap, which is a style that certain bikers wear, then my full-face helmet with a mirror tint shield, money in pocket, a lil' dope hidden well on me.

I can't explain the hiding place because I would being giving away information that the police still haven't caught on to, and though I am not into that scene or way of living today, I still know people that are. I'm still loyal as can be. I push that button and hear the pitter pat, pat pat, pat, pat, rumbling through the complex for about six minutes (warm up time), then my mind and my night train soft tail are W.F.O. to meet the guys. E.T.A. REAL QUICK.

I GET TO THE LIL' country music, jukebox-playing bar, and as usual, the guys are outside around the bikes, talking on the phone. The only thing was that Randy was arguing with someone. I assumed, of course, it was Lexi, but I was wrong! It was a dude that owed him money. It was only a hundred dollars, but I understand; it is the fucking principal. If you let one sleezy fucking fiend slip by, then they then you just as well give your dope away. So, how it goes? It goes like this. This dumb motherfucker on the other end of the phone claims that he ain't paying and if that's a problem, then meet him at the park. Really? Really? Well, guess what? Here we go in a split second, W.F.O.

PRESENT - October 24, 2015

I'm not too happy to write any of this. You must think I'm a haughty, selfish womanizer. Well, at one time, absolutely, no doubt that I was. I'm not a monster. I was just having fun by taking things to a new level. As I thought in my drug-dazed dizzy, contradicting my own contradictions, perceiving my own perception with the only consistent is my inconsistencies of a view, I sought but was the lone viewer. Aw, hell the drugs over a good period of time had diluted my affection for anything except when it comes down to my son Keaton. Not fair. I sometimes wonder that if he knew how much I depend on him for relief of my constant grief. It is not fair to have him hold that kind of bull shit, but I don't ever let him see my hurt just because there is none in his presence. Time is flying by in a phenomenal rate, and I don't want to miss any of it with him. I love him so and will never not. I'm forever his father and friend. He gives me his love in return, and it's so much purer than any other kind of love I have ever, ever experienced. You know, I know that he is the future, and I will raise him with respect for others and himself. We pray at night and praise when we awake for another day. He never knew or does he know the Kebee many have a story about. like night and day from the stickman to just a man, GOD fearing man,

October 25, 2015

Feeling magnificent! I'm leaping over boundaries and skipping through obstacles like a man with a cause. Maybe a cause that is prevalent.

The stickman, granted, it is hazardous, grim-fated, swift, and is depicted with the ability to only live in the past. Look, when I was in grade school, we were asked to write down on a sheet of paper what do we want to become, what we want to do as a career. I honestly did not know what I wanted to be. I thought for a couple of minutes and could hear whispers from other kids. "I gonna be a doctor, a fireman," and so on. I put a breadman, because my dad was a breadman, and he seemed happy, and we were well taken care of. The truth is, I wanted to be an outlaw of some sort. I wanted to live on the edge. I thought that's the way to be cool and recognized. I went from a kid playing with toys to a up-and-coming hustler of drugs and anything that was illegal, guns, etc., and, eventually, women for prostitution. I should have been a breadman like my dad! I was determined in any situation to be the last man standing. My key of never being setup or caught up with the long arm of the law was simply I had no M.O. I looked predictable, but I wasn't; I did shit on a whim. I knew bullshit when it was bullshit.

October 31, 2015

Had a good night with some longtime friends that I see only once a year, well, most of them. I went to pig roast that is put on by some good ol' boys. It's in the thirty-seventh year, had a difficult time being around a lot of people, due to my social disorder and paranoia. Things are just somehow in a diluted phase of a once joyful young man, turned into a lost substitutive satisfaction of who I formerly was. I don't know what I'm expecting to occur; maybe someone will bash me in the fucking head and clear my mind back to its comfort realm, or I will run into my next heartache. I'm battling this thought that ponders throughout my being. To be alone or to be in a relationship with one which I know will end like a train wreck and be alone again anyway, but the time in between, I'm not alone, and sure, there would have moments of peace and joy and companionship, then heartache; which is better?

CHAPTER 5
Kicking the Habit

As we are approaching the park to meet this tough guy that was on the other end of the phone that prompted this nerve awakening hurricane in my mind and gut. "Breathe, Kebee," I say to myself. You have to understand, I'm not a violent person per se; I'm a calm and, relative, peacemaker, unless I'm feeling that harm may be possibly done to me or my family. Then I will transform into a serious, diligent individual that has no fear of the very worst possible, meaning I go into battle prepared to die. Like anyone else, I don't want to die. So, that feeling of the will to survive taps into the ability to focus on eliminating the source that is your opponent, the enemy, the one that wants to take your life. When you channel that kind of energy and emotion, it will harness the strength of a dozen soldiers ready to unleash the fury within your vision, scanning the perimeter for anything or anyone else that could interfere with your now unstoppable mission to survive. This is what state of mind I'm in as I pull in behind Chad and Randy, because they didn't catch the stop light like I did, which put me behind a minute or so. This where I use the opportunity to light a cigarette. I'm always looking for the opportunity to light a smoke. Chad and Randy were off their bikes already, walking toward the motherfucker that has me in this mode to survive, and now it was inevitable that it was gonna be a fight. What a brave man this guy was. I respect him for keeping his word, and he was not just talking shit. He was ready to fight rather than pay; there is honor in that, to my way of thinking anyway.

I ride my bike past their bikes and then passed through the gate, barely fitting, which was a last call judgement that could have been an embarrassing moment that I would not have ever heard the end of it. I put on the brakes, causing a slide of the back tire pulling to the right, which was perfect to upon the complete stop put me in the position to kick my kick stand down at the same time. casually swing my right leg around to the left side of my bike to a perfect standing with my opportunist cigarette hanging out my mouth. Now, I'm very protective of my younger brother and also with certain friends. I rather me get hurt than them. I built up a high tolerance for pain through the years, mainly through a work-related accident in 1995. I was caught in an explosion that caused second and third degree burns on over 40 percent of my body, including my face. The whole process of treating these burns consists of being submerged in a whirlpool of warm water and being scrubbed like you would be sanding down an old painted piece of wood, peeling the skin right off of your swollen flesh. There are no examples to describe this treatment, something a person never forgets, never would feel pain like that again. I don't think there is any pain compared to these burns. I would pray to God to never let any of my loved ones ever feel this kind of suffering and to go ahead and give all their pain to me right then and there. Never, ever want them to feel something to the magnitude.

As we are approaching this guy, to whom I recognized, and a couple of his friends he brought along, I hear him saying, as I get closer to engaging a mixture of skills of martial arts that I learned and adapted too, "Like fish can swim." I was taught by a variety of guys that were ranked in the martial arts as black belts and some even higher degrees of black belt. I used what they taught me and put my own style mix with it, and it became very useful over the years and very affective and utilized through discipline and payed off with accuracy. The words he was mumbling were in audible to my ears. He was attempting to hand me what he said was half the money. So, with his reached out right hand with cash in it, I reached out with my right hand at a distance where I was able to hold his hand like we were shaking hello, but I held it firmly and used it like a counter balance, then executed a snap kick right to the head, and as he began to fall, being that I still had his hand, I snapped back my right leg to the ground. I held him up, and his eyes were wandering, trying to focus. Now, the craziest thing occurred as I snapped kick him; my smoke in my mouth fell out because of the force I applied, which caused my head to tilt to the left, but as it fell in synchronicity as the kick, I caught it with my left hand, right between my middle finger and index finger, and quickly put it back in my mouth, like I had meant for that to happen, but no, it just happened and fell into my hand, purely luck. So, I played it off as I was that cool and took a drag off it and said, "Keep the other half of the money, but don't ever come around me or my family ever again." Shit like that was just in my favor that day. He and his little entourage quietly walked away with their heads down as Randy and Chad stood each on a side of me with their chest bowed out like a momma bear protecting her family. The truth was that I didn't give thought to what I was gonna do; it just happened that way, and my hands were shaking, and I felt like I was gonna throw up right in the presence of these fucking jack offs, causing all these emotions running through me and an adrenaline high that was almost to intoxicating.

"Breathe, Kebee," I say silently. I get nervous as hell in these moments. That is the truth; I just hide very well.

So, that was that, and we were standing around looking at each other with these shit-eating grins, kinda halfhearted smiles. The ordeal ended just as quick as it begun, and it all unfolded to our favor. It will be night soon, and I still needed to get to the weed at the house in the basin. We calm down and plan our route and discuss the speed we are gonna ride at. It's gonna be W.F.O. OR low and slow like a Sunday sightseeing voyage. We agreed to take it slow; we don't want to push our luck and be big-headed after the victory we just made out with. You know, no one got seriously injured or for a matter of fact got killed. So, we pull out on our way to the basin. I can't wait to get there and relax and roll a bowl of meth to get the receptors in my brain communicating at the rate of which now I'm believing it is normal thinking speed, kinda like turning on all the lights and anything that plugs to an outlet in your house and get the meter turning at a fast rotation. I need my receptors talking to one another.

November 2, 2015

I'm back with the fucking trivia of this world, spitting out my mouth while curling my tongue sideways, trying to hold back the words that are too cynical for these backwoods anal fucking retards. This is why I stay home on these nights. I'm suffering with my schizophrenic paranoia in its peak, running for solitude.

Lord Jesus, please fight this for me. Life has become stagnant for me, believing I may possibly be a sociopath. I can't be that. I need to focus on what is most important.

Yes, Keaton, my baby boy, really not a baby anymore, but he is my baby. Its just life is always waiting to be next, always in line waiting and ordering a large only to get a small, and if you don't notice that right away, guess what, to the back of the fucking line. I swear this what has become of the world. ALWAYS waiting in a fricking line or on hold, hearing that your call is important to them, and your wait time is approximately two minutes. Yeah right! I'm so overwhelmed at this particular moment. I need peace of mind and meditation and spend some time in my prayer closet on my knees.

November 3, 2015

I'm reminded of what the meaning of "living on the edge" is to me. The stickman philosophy is "you can't live on the edge until you have been over the edge before."

This is how you can live on the edge and not fall over, only because you now recognize your limit and boundaries that have been set by the collapse of your first attempt of living on the edge. Timing is an incontestable fact, the past is incorrigible, the present is perplexed, and the future is not determined. Right place at the right time or the wrong place at the wrong time! All depends on how you look at the situation. I'm browsing through Walmart today, and I decided to look at some jewelry before I left. This was a last second decision that caused me to go across the whole store when I was already at the exit. Not sure why I done this. Timing, I tell you, Bam! I hear, "Look, Kebee," and I immediately recognize this voice, although it has been quite a while since I heard her voice. Well, it's my friend in the flesh. TESSIE, man, I needed some joy badly, and a great big hug, then another hug as we say goodbye. It was great to see her, and she was with her pride and joy, "her son." It was just small talk, but I love her energy and really that was the second encounter of the day that gives me happiness and hope. When my old friend Cotton Gin TIM gives me a visit this morning, timing, I tell you, is everything! And good friends are an essential part for me, now that I'm mostly living a phlegmatic kind of way. They sure changed that way, for today anyway. Thank you, Jesus, for I know it's not in my time, but in your timing, not my will, but your will.

November 4, 2015

So much in life has a both negative and a positive impact of who I am today. I'm told often "Don't worry," but I do anyway. Like a turtle, I go in and out of my shell. What did I do to myself? Do I really want the answer? That's the million-dollar question. Do I want the truth about myself? It is there inside of me, in me deeply rooted, that I ignore daily. I can't be the only one to feel this way, could I? I see a shrink twice a year, and sometimes I want to tell her everything that my mind believes and has absorbed, but all that will do is getting myself hospitalized for weeks. You know, that might be the vacation of solitude I need. Who is controlling this human depth finder? It is a power beyond my description, pulling the stickman back to the surface for air to breathe.

It the world prepared for the release of this kind of varmint? How humble must I be before I explode? Haven't I been humble enough? I'm a fricking time bomb with no time. I'm a fucking dud, poof, nothing but a cloud of smoke. I become harmless, a dog that is just bark, then not even really all bark. I'm silent, watching and observing the rise and collapse of these mutants that are imitating the stickman. Wake up, Kebee, come back, Kebee, is what I hear in my head. Tormenting me constantly with a level of high-pitched ringing in my ears. So, I just sit and smile!

CHAPTER 6
Headlight

Okay, we made the ride to the basin safely. It was a nice, easy, scenic ride. I like those putt-putt rides; they can be just what the doctor ordered for the stressful life we are defined to. As we are taking off our helmets, I notice Chad and Randy giggling like two little girls and looking at me. Now, I already know what the giggles are about. You see, about six months back, I was in the area, and I was tired from a three-day adventure, of course, "on a meth high," and the young lady we know her as "Star," she is the dark loner, deep talker, dressed always like a modern-day witch. It's her attribute to be called a witch. Well, I'm just say that I am positive in my mind this is what happened, but no one believes me, and Star denies this event of ever happening. Okay, I'm tired, so I decided to go there; I knew it would be cool. She's like part of thc gang, per se. I get there, she greets me at the door, and welcomes me like always. It didn't take long before I was falling out while we were in a conversation. Mainly, she did all the talking, because I gave what I had left on me about a half gram. I make my way to the couch from the kitchen. and within a minute I was out, only to be awakened by Star sitting on top of my lap, pouring Jack Daniel's whiskey on my bare chest, with the blinds open just enough for the moonlight to shine in. I mean, it's a fricking curse this witch is performing on me, like I'm a circus freak or something. She calmly pushes me back down with her hand on my chest till I was lying flat on my back. She's telling me, "It's okay, trust me; I'm not gonna hurt you." Well, you know what? I aint been fucking right since then. Good witch, my ass!

"Go ahead and laugh it up, guys. I'm telling y'all she did something," I say with a smile, because it is crazy when you tell it out loud. I should have never told them two anyway, but I am really uncomfortable around Star now, because its either true and that's fucking scary enough, or its not and I'm looking like an idiot, embarrassed. I guess the explanation would be, in my defense, down in the south, around these parts, voodoo is a religion to many. It is possible that I dreamed it also. More like a nightmare. "Hey, guys," rings out off of the front porch as always there to greet anyone that stops by. There ain't a whole lot of action going on in these parts. Isolation is a good way to describe this way of life out here in the basin. They love company, but it's far and few between visitors. "'Sup?" Randy shouts as we are walking up the porch. "Want some Jack, Kebee," Star says with her giggling her sarcasm. "Fuck you, Star," is my comeback. How original. It's getting late, and I'm eager to grab the rest of the pot, but first, I'm gonna do a line and smoke a bowl, because I believe I need it. That's the way it is for me, always looking for the opportunity to get high, well, get higher, if that is even possible. With that being done, I'm ready to move on with my plan. "Where is the weed, Star?" She goes in the back room with a duffle bag and throws it next to my feet. I wasn't prepared to see this compacted weed in one fucking solid block! This a problem for me because of its bulkiness. It's one large block; how am I gonna put this on my bike? I brainstorm for a minute. Boom. "Star, do you have a saw?" "Check the shed," she replies, so we all three of us guys go to the shed, and while looking for a saw, we all tweaked the fuck out, start talking about everything that was of no relation to finding a saw. We were in that shed for at least two hours before we found a saw. The funny thing is no one asked me why I needed a saw. I assume that they were thinking what I was thinking.

With the saw now in my custody, we go back to the house, grab the block of weed, and put in the tub, and I start saw the block in pieces. Let me tell you, this weed was compressed like it was vacuumed airtight. After about an hour of sawing the weed into three separate blocks, I put them each in their own trash bag, wrapped it up real tight, and went strap it to my backrest of my bike. Randy and Chad do the same also; they wrapped a shirt around the bag for the reason not to look suspicious. Dammit, now I want to do the same, so I ask Star for and old shirt or clothing while I unstrap the block from my backrest. I'm tweaked the hell out. My mind is going faster than my bodily motions, as if I had sound effects to every movement. If I move my arms, then you hear eeeeeek, standing up, rrrrrrk, coming out my mouth, it's like I'm animated and have the sound effects that come with it. Man, I'm tweaked, and I'm not the only one either. After Star brings me a shirt to wrap my block of weed like the two geniuses, I am riding home dirty with… On second thought of this journey, back to Lafayette. I'm envisioning the whole fucking scene of getting stopped, and we understand that this is possible. I discussed this many times with several different people, my dope! I will be the one that pulls over and the rest of the pack hits it W.F.O and never looks back. All you have to do is hit a side road and stash the stash, just in case they call for back up, but they will take what they can get without endangering lives. Me, I will pull over and take the charge. That's the law the code we go by.

We tell Star goodbye as we start up the bikes. We zip up our jackets, put on the helmets, then the gloves, ready to roll out. Wrong, just out of the driveway Randy stops, so me and Chad stop and wait while watching him from our mirrors and notice his headlight is not working. Remember, we are in the basin on a levee road. There are no streetlights, and homes and camps are a good bit of distance from one another. It's fucking pitch black out there. I'm ready to abort this mission.

FUCK MAN, why now? I ask myself, I'm telling you this is the work of a witch and her curse. So, here we are, in the driveway, close to the levee road, and we are trying to figure out the problem. Well, the fucking problem is there is a mile of electrical tape around the wiring to start with. Too many fucking hands been on this bike.

Here I am in the dark, with Chad and Randy shinning a flashlight in the area of where the problem may be. The problem is, they can't stop moving from side to side and I'm still making sound effects to my movements. What a show that we are putting on. A coon-ass operation at its best. We spent a couple of hours trying to figure out where the short maybe was, but due to the excessive electrical tape wrapped around the wiring, it was a battle, and it was obvious we weren't going to find it. Now, being so protective of Randy, I came up with a plan, a solution to the problem. "Give me some of the tape wrapped around the wiring, and also y'alls flashlights." Then I taped the flashlights to the handlebars, then instructed them to follow closely behind me, with Randy on my bike and me on his in front. This way, if each were on a side, one to the rear left and then the other to the rear right, they would produce light for me along with the two flashlights I mounted.

This is going to work out, so we start out once more, now really late, and a bitter chill is in the wind. Fuck it, I been cold before, and I'm sure I'll be cold again. Everything is working like as planned, although we could not go W.F.O., but as we cross the Patoon Bridge, a bridge that's rising and lowers upon the water level.as so as I hit a bump on the raggedy bridge the fucking headlight started working. What a pleasure to see. I'm not sure that they could notice it was working, so I just continued on the way we were. The funny thing is that it seemed like were going a hundred miles per hour, and in my mirror, I could see cars coming around Randy and Chad. Then, on the side of me, passing us up, and they almost seemed like they were floating by us and we were all going uphill, but I know this road, and it does not go up hill. I'm freaking out a little. Something is strange, and it felt as if we were not making any progress to getting to the next lil' town. The time it takes is about ten to fifteen minutes, but I was sure somehow we were on a different road. "It couldn't be," I'm saying to myself. WTF, I'm tripping bad, which is making me even higher than I was. My nerves were rattled. Were we in some kind of time warp? This was absolutely out of this world, and I was out of my mind. Then, as another car passes me, I look at my speedometer, and I was leading the three of us at a record speed, a fast 25 mph maxed to 30, then again dropped to 25mph. Man, wow, it seemed we were flying. We get to the gas station in the lil' town. I stopped, not for gas, but to catch my head. And, boy, I tell you the truth, Chad and Randy felt and thought exactly as I did, so it wasn't just me feeling the weird experience. As we are discussing these events, a, on-duty police car pulls into the parking lot a few yards from us. "Be cool, ya'll," I say under my breath, hoping he is just making his routine rounds and he will go about his patrol. No, he gets out the cruiser, starts walking in our direction, and is looking right at us, then stop at the store's front doors and says, "Kinda chilly out there, huh, guys?" So Chad being the mediator of the group, he can talk to anyone about anything any subject and always ending that they have a mutual friend, every fucking time; hey, it's a grand gift to have. "Yes, sir, but we love to ride any chance we can." The officer gently replies with, "Y'all be careful on them roads." All three said with a shit-eating grin, "Thanks, sir, you too." Needless to say, we didn't stick around to see him come out of the store. I was so nervous that I could not find my key to my bike, and in a panic, I start slapping my pockets to feel for them. They could not be far. I didn't go but two feet from my bike the whole time. Randy and Chad have their bikes in gear, and they are ready to take off. They are puzzled, just staring, making hand motions to what I assumed were "what the fuck?" So, I pulled my helmet off to start to tell them my dilemma, and bam, my keys fall to the ground. Shit, I forgot I put them in my helmet and was so nervous that I quickly put my helmet on and never took them out. The weird thing is I didn't feel them resting on my head, probably because it was cold, and I was scared! I hurried and started Randy bike, and we shot out of there. Sheeewww, that was a close one. Can't wait to get back on our side of town, and I have a date with Heather in about eighteen hours from then. It's all good, and I couldn't wait to tell them that, "I told y'all she is a voodoo witch or something," meaning the weird ride and the light not working and all, but when we got home, I didn't say anything. It's best not to even put that in their mind and have them fucked in the head like me.

November 8

Like I always say, "Fucking physic vampires scattered all over." They are in every nook and cranny, in search for the essence of a person.

Here I am, lonely and waiting in love, and in love with waiting. I can't grasp the swift way of the world. Am I just that ignorant? Am I the only one without the ability to understand what is prevalent by the world and the mutants in it? I spend my days in fear of the rejection of the society that I'm trapped in. I believe that I'm just frequently misunderstood in my attempts to fit in with anyone on a prevailing social environment. I was once told that I fit in anywhere but belong to no one permanently.

I am more aggravated today than any other time to my recollection. No particular reason at all, just everything is working my nerves on overtime. I find myself chasing clues that may or may not be. Is there something I'm trying to figure out? I don't know, but things feel not right, period. I can't stop my mind from its paranoia. I'm looking for answers to things that may not be happening in reality. I'm struggling for my sanity from its insanity, its massive madness in its best spectacular moments. These moments are real. Even if it's an illusion, it is real to me. I can't tell what is reality or an illusion. This is my daily struggle, and I seem to remember that I put myself through this game of some sort. Do I ask questions?

Or do I just sit and observe and figure out the craziness? I'll never know, and maybe that's best, because I'm chasing my own tail. It's nothing, it's nothing; it's all in my mind. This is what I have to do not to hurt myself or anyone else. "It's nothing, Kebee," I keep saying over and over. Then I will have some quiet time of meditation. Right now, I need it right now. GOD HELP ME!

RANDOM WRITINGS

woke up this morning a little too fast, spilling yesterday's drink out of a half empty glass
the hands on the clock are in reverse as time moves in forward motion
let me tell you, this slick guy ain't sipping none of her voodoo potions

when you seen it all of what matters
you kinda lose touch but still able to feel
as you march through the trenches for the very last kill.
when knowledge is gained from the strong by the weak
promising you what you sow you will one day reap

friends that are truly the enemy, raping, robbing, stealing your peace
closing the door upon your release

These are lyrics from three different songs I have written lately. I love writing songs; maybe one day I will sell one.

That's a dream of mine. Yeah, I would like to give this world back something out of my craziness and hurt from my self-destruction.

November 11, 2015

In the midst of the dark vast emptiness, I am stuck in a blue mood that won't disappear. I'm reminded of the hurt and lost I experienced through this wicked world we are presently residing. I imagine my self being hurdled through the empty void of space to escape my demons. Don't get me wrong, I have everything to be grateful for, and I count my blessings. It's just ridiculously evident that I could have done better in life, but it is what it is. I try to be aware of opportunities that I encounter daily and utilize my chances at living better than I once did in the not-so-distant past. I do know this; people do and can change. The other night, my cousin Danny called me to invite me to a get together at this lil' bar for his birthday. I was glad to hear from him it had been a while since we have seen one another. We are very close and were raised as brothers more than cousins. We are very close, and we have many legendary stories to tell. I'm not gonna get into that, but I went meet him, and I knew ahead of time that there would be these new friends of his that he recently been spending his time with, including some women. That really motivated me, to meet some new chicks. I get there, and they are already into their third or fourth drink, laughing and shooting the shit. I approach and give him a big hug, and he introduces me to all them, then whispers to me which one of these hot chicks he was trying to make time with. Wouldn't you know it, it was my first choice, and I was extremely attracted to the same one as him. I, of course, backed off, not even making eye contact with her for the remainder of the evening.

Let first make this clear me and Danny are like brothers and are both fueled by our love of narcotics as it had been since I was at the impressionable age of thirteen. That's what we know; that was the protocol, getting high, but we both changed our lifestyles, him more than me. I have detachment issues by letting go of people that still live the seedy life of crime and drugs. I love these people; they been with me forever. I can't just walk away. They been loyal always, and I stay loyal to them. I just don't partake in the activity of that way of life. Here I am, witnessing my cousin with his new friends and watching the actions of a bonded group of individuals converse on basic normalities of life. I'm an alien to these people; I didn't fit in anywhere, on any subject they pondered.

I was out of place with one of the closest persons in my entire life! So, after an hour or so, I announced I was heading out; no one really heard me. I politely interrupted their circle of debates and hugged Danny, and we exchanged I love yous. I looked him directly in the eyes and knew that he will never be in my life as it always was before. I'm happy for him. He struggled throughout his life, trying to find some clarity and purpose. It was bittersweet walking out that joint. An era has ended. I have no words to describe the emotions, only he made it out, alive! Sometimes I put all my issues in a wheelbarrow, my addictions, my hurt, my problems, all my sinful ways, all that kept me with fear and grief, all that kept me strapped down in life. I took this wheelbarrow of terror to GOD and said, "Take this, all this, Lord," and turned and walked away. After about two or more steps, i turned, filled with anxiety and said, "Wait, I need this, and I need that," I couldn't let it all go, at least I gave some, and I believe "GOD understands," because I am who I am by the grace of GOD!

CHAPTER 7

Whose Dog?

Finally, this abstract trio of misfits make back to the complex where we live. What a pleasure and great relief to see my townhome. We unstrap the pot from our bike with a stressful look that is starting to subside into a gentle breath of accomplishment. I climb in the attic again and put all the shit together and climb down to join the guys, kicking back with some good ol' rock and roll in the living room; light the torch and roll the dice. Now, in the euphoric realm of numbness of reality that collapse the chaos of the fast-moving unsettling life we endure, self-inflicted by our own choice. The hour is hitting the three A.M.; what to do? I don't have to deliver the goods till anytime between noon and six P.M. .I'm nowhere close to being sleepy as I ponder this as ten other intruding thoughts race around my mind all at once. my phone rings. It's a couple college girls who I met in the complex a week or so ago; they recently moved here, and we hit it off by kinda hinting what our poison was, without saying it bluntly. Bottom line, hey, they like to party. I answer in a calm tone, "Hey, beautiful." Now, I'm gonna let go of a couple of my foolproof pick up techniques. I wink to Randy and Chad and mouth silently, "Pay attention to this!" "Hey, Ashley!" Now, the thing is, I know her name is Renee. Okay, when you ask a woman her name, and especially when they are magazine beautiful and they know that they are, you wait a standard ten to fifteen minutes and call her a name that is not even close to her name. Boom. They are in shock and disbelief that you don't remember her name, because she is almost famously beautiful, and this never happens to them, okay, you follow? Now they become perplexed by this wave of anger, and in their pretty little head is thoughts of "Who the fuck is this guy to not remember my name?" And strangely, you now become a mystery that has to be solved by them committing themselves to making sure you will never forget her name again. Trust me, you then have their full attention and focus on you, so they can redeem the blow to their shallow confidence that you just kicked in the twat. Warning: do not try it more than once; you will give yourself away. Now you can hesitate one time a few minutes later when you engage again in a conversation; you know, kind of squint your eyes, hold your finger up, and blurt out her real name, as if you just burnt in your brain forever. I'm telling you, man, works every fricking time, but hey, of course, that's just the ice breaker; you need to have more game ready to spit out in a moment's notice. Okay, I'll give you another, then that's all I can let go of. Start and direct the conversation towards how inconsiderate men can be to their girlfriends and how there are not many gentlemen left these days. I guarantee that she will have a story of some idiot she had a date with. So, after you hear about the poor slop, you nail this with passion! I tell you, "You know, I always treat my dates, and women in general, as I want my mother and little sister to be treated!" And, for the record, truly in agreement with this line, so I'm not just spitting the game, for the record, but this will melt them right in front of your eyes, knowing they can't wait to tell their own mother the next day how she met a great guy and tell her what you said. So, there you go, my free pick up line to every guy that is reading this.

Ashley, "Mymy name is not Ashley."

"Oh, I thought?"

"Fuck you, asshole; it's Renee!"

"Yes, yes, so sorry, Renee. I'll never make this mistake again." When they curse you like in an embarrassed sort of manner, they have taken the bait, and you got them on the hooked now, just reel them in slowly. I'm high and I'm rather witty and humorous to cover up the introvert that I really am. I ask Renee what I could do for her, and she rambles a bit about how she heard the bike pull into the complex and so on. Then she gets to the point and tells a story of how her and Charrie, her roommate, who is the more reserved of the pair, that they were still up and were decorating their apartment and it would be cool if I wanted to go hang out. "Well," I reply, "I have my friend and brother that are with me, is that still cool?" As I'm saying this, I'm raising my brows at my two compadres. She tells me no problem; they would love the company. I tell Renee we would be there in a half hour or so. Randy announces to me as I hang up that he was gonna pass on the invite and go home to his family, that he has had enough of the stickman for one night. We all give a loud outburst of laughter. You see, in the time we were back at the house in the basin, when we were looking for tools in the shed but ended up rambling off ideas and just plain gibberish, Chad came up with a cool little epiphany as he described it; that everywhere we go, somewhere, mainly the restroom, we agreed was the best location to do our tribute to the stickman. This is a simple attribute we are trying to create by drawing a stickman, a small stickman, all over the town, like restaurants and clubs, even homes. This is an experiment just to see how many places we go when were not together to try and see if we have been there and left a stickman. Maybe this will catch on and when you are wiping your mouth in a nice restaurant, maybe in the corner of the cloth napkin, you might see a little stickman. Do you dig the concept? Naturally, we will get a few more mutants to join in the experiment.

Randy is walking out the door, giving a wave and gesture of see you later as I explain to Chad about meeting Renee and Charrie a few days earlier, and how we hit it off and we were both profiling each other, with the mutual result of we all like to party, so on and so on, and we exchanged numbers as I was adamant in doing so by expressing that if they needed anything, I mean anything at all, I'm right down the row from them and would be of help if needed. That made the girls feel safe a bit; well, I like to think it did. Anyway, I got her number, and she got mine, so me and Chad take off walking to their apartment and not even worried we haven't cleaned up in almost two days, and we are going meet these two hot chicks, and I'll tell you why it didn't matter that we been rolling around in the same clothes all this time, with our oily hair and stubble on our face, dirt under our nails, and dirty clothes. The reason is not because we didn't believe in good personal hygiene, because we did bring toothbrushes everywhere we would go, there are two things that tell you a lot about a person, and that's their teeth and their shoes. My mom was always drilling her kids to brush our teeth, and your footwear kind of gives a hint to who you are. It all boils down to this; CONFIDENCE WITHOUT ANY COMPROMISE! Then you know this; women want to be noticed, bottom line. Notice your girl or the one you are in pursuit of, simply notice these beautiful beings. Now, you throw in a good wingman, and you should have no resistance from the women species. Chad I come to believe he thinks he is my wingman, but in retrospect, I am his, due to the fact this guy can talk to anyone in any situation! He is a great conversationalist and a perfect gentleman that will listen and never try and interrupt till that other person has finished. I admire that, because I have a fucking motor mouth. this is one of my great many flaws. On the walk to these girls' apartment townhome, I bet Chad that they are tweaked and decorating their new place. I mean it's like four thirty in the morning. Who else is up and wants the company of misfits? And not just decorating, but decorating the whole place with dollar store décor, when I blurted out that vision. We laughed like some cackling hens as we are approaching the door. "One dollar, Chad," I say, "One dollar is the bet."

I knock, and the door opens with Renee standing there with some little blue jean cutoffs and a tight spaghetti shirt, low cut, with her dark black hair that enhances her deep blue eyes. I love dark-haired ,dark-complexion women. She is holding the door open as me and Chad pick up our jaws that just hit the ground. Then, as we entered, I'm thinking what I know Chad is thinking, "Why we didn't clean up a lil'?" It seems I must have been in a haze of sleep-deprived vision when I first met these young ladies, toddling down the stairs in an equally jaw-dropping beauty is Charrie, all smiles around the room. As we scan the freshly decorated place, I tap Chad on the shoulder as we were invited to make ourselves at home. "You owe me a dollar." As much I would like to tell you in detail about the next eight to nine hours, I can't, but I can say that there was some ecstasy and smoking and eating chards of meth, indulging in abundance. I can tell you just a blur of remembrance of Chad standing on a Dollar Store white plush shag rug and leaving his road grime from the bottom of his boots. I acted fast and rolled it up and threw it behind the couch in fear of stink now with the perspiring flesh caused from our indulging appetite. Chad finds a can of Lysol and sprays us down, which did make the stink worse. I assume this because they stayed upstairs for a good part of time we were there. The ecstasy was really rolling me into a fetal position with the loss of all my confidence and began to compromise all. This shit had me. It wasn't till the screams of "Whose fucking dog?" rang down from upstairs. It seems that a few moments earlier, when I heard a thump against the door, I took upon myself with the triple vision that I was experiencing to open the door and let in a dog which, for some reason, I was sure it was theirs only because

Chad said to let the dog in. They have a dog. I saw the pictures of them and a dog. I should have asked to describe it, but man, we were out the box. Well, it wasn't, and the dog was running in a panic through the place, and I just froze. My mind would not relate to my legs or any other part of my body to do anything. After that, I was disoriented and was in somehow bent down in front of my place petting a cat. I have no recollection of leaving these girls who have broken me and will probably laugh at me for the remainder of their existence. Now I'm unsure why I stopped to pet this feline in front my house or how long I was doing this strange out-of-character display of emotions towards a stray pet. It was only when I snapped back into the dimension I know and believe to be the fleshly one here on Earth, by the sound of my neighbor's voice repeating, "Kebee, Kebee, what you doing? Are you okay?" The look upon his face was puzzled with a smile when I looked up at him, away from the cat. I stand up and switch into a cool tone with a, "Just chilling."

He chuckles and says, "All right, man; be cool, Kebee, and take it easy, my man." I just kind of nod with a little wave as turn my attention back to the pussycat.

This shit really fucked my head up, because now all I see is a Subway bag, no cat! I was petting a Subway bag. All I could do is think, "Good thing my neighbor is cool," and laughed to myself. I get inside my place as quickly as I could put the key in the door and slide in and leave that gree-gree outside. there was no sign of Chad, and I don't have any idea when and how we got separated. This happens; we know we are grown men and are well. No news is good news.

I flop myself down on the sofa and start peeling off my clothes, first kicking off the boots, then trying to wiggle out of the leather pants. About halfway through my struggle, I lay back and just think about different scenes I been on, and I come to this conclusion; drugs are not a problem! It's a social disturbance that will take you places you don't want to go and keep you there longer than you want to stay! How is all this chaos gonna end? I ponder, Is this the final stage of the social system that I am no longer able to maintain as I once did? Is this the entropy? The drugs are having a different affect to what was the usual epitome. I knew right there GOD KNEW THEN how much I would love him in the future. I felt it; my life would start to shift in a different direction. I was experiencing a peace and calm that was unfamiliar to me. I was okay with being embarrassed over being out done by them two beautiful mutants earlier. I have done nothing in this world that made a difference up to this point, not a good, positive difference. I will be forgotten. Who am I? Who will even remember? Maybe someone will remember something good and not just an outlaw. These are the thoughts I pondered before I passed out into a deep sleep.

November 17, 2015

They say that if you want to find out if you are a good leader, then just look behind you and see who is following you. The world is gasping for its last breathes, it seems to me. There is terror daily, the media is displaying the fantastically intriguing images of what is putting the fear into us mutants. But is this daily broadcast just to keep us in fear? Would the government lie and embellish the story of tragic events? Well, I'm not gonna be fed and feed off the fear. I'm gonna do what is what everyone should, practice through the panic and chaos, look to be persevering with all an optimistic point of veiw. Love thy neighbor as thy love thyself. Build a relationship with the good Lord and establish a direct line to him. Pray that he may be merciful on your soul and forgive you for your many sins. Amen!

> I turned a new leaf off a broken branch of an old tree
> that grew from misery and pain with lots of grief.
> gained some wisdom and renewed belief
> let's just keep it between you and me!

I'm still waiting in love, and now in love with waiting. There is a bad storm out tonight. I guess I'm riding it out alone; who am I fooling? I'm riding every night alone. I bring myself to tears when I look back and all the shit I put myself through and my family through. It wasn't worth it! I could have been anything I wanted. All I wanted was to be a hustler and live the in the underworld. Through it all, it made me who I am today, "a nobody," other than a father, and I'm better at that than I ever was as a hustler. I just wish I would have some other accomplishments to pass down to Keaton. I know he loves me and will continue to love me no matter what I have. Man, I love him. Thank you, Lord!

CHAPTER 8
And the Luck of the Stickman

"Sounds of Silence" by Simon and Garfunkel, is how I feel is the experience of the stickman. Yeah, a song written before my time is a song that whispers understanding of what may be the belief of what is real to me in my spinning thoughts. Music is what moves me; it's my happiness, my sadness, it's my memory of special moments. I'm in a deep sleep but aware of the music coming out the stereo, playing my disc of my favorites, and I jump up screaming, "What the fuck? How long have I been sleeping?" One look at the number of voicemails on my phone, and I know to way to long. It's eleven o'clock, New Year's Eve. I never made the delivery of weed, and now I'm way too late to bring in the New Year with Heather; that I was so looking forward to spending it with her. I try numerous times, and she will not answer my call. I'm really bummed, really! So, I got go make this drop off. I grab the weed and jump in my truck and haul ass across town, trying not to break too many laws, and what do I do? Run a red fucking light! Taking a right-hand turn and didn't make a complete stop before making the turn. The drop off was one block away. I'm looking at the actual house when the strobe and blue lights in my mirror are flashing from behind. So, I turn in to a store parking lot, thinking, "This it. I finally got caught." I was sure this was it. The worst situation to find yourself in.

The patrol car comes around me on the left side and does a U-turn in the parking lot. Now he is facing the front of my vehicle, front bumper to bumper, sort of speak, with a few feet between us. He calls out on the loudspeaker and directs me to exit the vehicle as he shines the blinding bright spotlight.

I'm completely in a blank state of mind. I had no excuse I could come up with due to the damage of my brain from the past two weeks of a drug and alcohol matrimony. I'm fucked. I look like what I am, "an addicted burnout" that has pushed the boundaries of a magnificent carnival act in its time of losing the ability to continue the production. "Buck up," I whisper to myself, "Smile, you ignorant mutant." So, I heard my words but could not put them to use. What will my mug shot say about me? "What a disappointment to society," the words will read under my picture. The officer approaches with the usual protocol," License and registration, please."

"Yes, sir," I reply, then he recaps the whole reason of the illegal turn that now has us in this horrible interaction. "Run," I think, but my condition that I'm currently in will not get me anything but out of breath and probably a behind the scenes ass whipping. At this point, I'm ready to just get this ordeal over with. The officer asks the question, "Been drinking tonight?" "A couple shots out the bottle in my vehicle." He gonna find the whiskey that I was sipping down to try and get in the mood of New Year's anyway, which was in about thirty minutes till midnight. I'm thinking, "Man, Heather is never gonna want to see me again." This is heavy, because I really wanted to start something good and new with her. So, he takes my license and tells me, "stand in front of my vehicle," and walks over to his cruiser, and gets in but keeping the spotlight and his eye on me while he runs my name through the system. Then, a miracle; it's the only explanation. Why do I deserve a miracle? I can't really give any logical answer to that!

This event was a life-altering event. I mean I was looking at least a year in jail if the officer would have checked my truck, which was about to become my worst fear, and reality has made its presence known. All of a sudden, I hear a loud screeching sound, getting louder by the second. This sound was painfully similar to fingernails scratching down a chalkboard, but loud, I tell you. I turn and look towards the main road, and I see bright orange traces of what seemed like sparks from someone grinding metal. Then, as this roaring screech is just about in my view, I turn and look back at the officer sitting in his cruiser, and he had this puzzled look just like I had. Then it appears right in front of us, passing on the main road; its a truck, an older model Ford with no tires. I mean just the rims digging down into the pavement, no rubber on the rims, and throwing sparks behind him like a comet in outer space, and to top it off, there is a pole sticking through and out of the windshield, and the driver is laughing and waving his hand up and down like he is on a rollercoaster ride in Disney World. The officer is now pulling his cruiser right beside me with my license in his hand, sticking out his window. He says, "Son, get to where you going, and I don't want to see you on the road again tonight." I reached out to grab my license and registration with an uninitiated robotic movement of my phlegmatic body with sound effects and all, "weeee annnnannn," and say, "Now, he is fucked up." I mean, who in the hell is this lucky? Well, that night it was me, as I watched the officer go in pursuit of a madman, that saved my ass!

I take off in total amazement to my destination, roaring with excitement to share this story to anyone who would want to hear about my luck. Well, when I get there and listen to the gripping of where the hell I been? So, I tell them the story, and everyone laughed and didn't believe that what I was telling had no truth to it at all. So, here I am, bringing in the new year, 2006, with a group of mutants! This is what is running through my mind as they count down. What I did next is without any apprehension at all; I pick up a more than half-full fifth of vodka and turn it up and kill it without even taking a breath. Now, due to this act of being plain out don't give a fuck, I am not exactly clear on the next six hours. I wake up on the floor which was spinning till I caught my focus. I realized that, once again, I have made a complete fool of myself. So, I stumble to the restroom. As I walk past a few party goers passed out in different positions scattered across the living room, I got to throw up first, then take a piss. Now, the throwing up I can explain, but the shocker of the attempt to piss is very perplexing. You see, I had a condom on, a green condom. WTF? Let's just move on, because I don't know, and maybe don't need to know! So, as I clean up the piss all over, due to the condom still on my dick, flush the bastard down the drain, then I take a makeup pencil, is what I call it, and take the opportunity to draw a small stickman where the wall and ceiling meet above the toilet. This now jogs my brain to, where is Chad? And, at that moment, my phone goes off in the walky-talky mode, "Hey, brah, what's your twenty?" Damn, it's Chad. You see, I always had the gift of seeing around corners. I just never figured out the fundamentals of applying any ability to utilize the gift, so I just watch the moments unfold as I knew they would, as they pass easy on by.

December 1, 2015

I am part of the problem still to this very day. Sure, I made changes, but not enough! The world has gone mad, I'm telling you! I have not done anything to change the world for the better. If I did, I take no credit for it. I guess you can say I'm like a homeless dog licking my wounds. Me and my closest friends have no interest in politics of the world. I mean what does it take to conform to society? Freedom is doing exactly what you want to do but have no fear in doing it. I yet found freedom in any one person to this date. What are you afraid of? For me, it's not dying, it's living a life while crying!

December 2, 2015

blah blah blah

December 4

How do I go on with this grand production of the stickman? We live in a world of chaos and compromise, all to fit our needs as we see it. I'm not feeding into the whole process of the egotistic relationship of the world, but I guess I don't see myself as others do ,or do I even have a reflection in mirror with a proper description? I could be blind, or even mentally retarded, and not know it. Does anyone ever tell a mentally handicapped person that he is mentally handicapped? I think not. We play along as if we are the equal to them! So, you can be in this condition and not even know your different. So be it! I don't care. I love myself either way. Although I began to realize that I like being sad, and I like to cry, I'm alright with this emotion. It makes it even better when I do experience the joys of life, and I do have more joy than sadness.

It's been confirmed to me over and over only GOD, only truly GOD, can do these things, things that you can't understand but know something is not what it seems to be! Mercy me, mercy me, I'm not worthy, Lord, but thank you, thank you for always showing me the way. Search my heart; what have I missed to make it through my trials and tribulations? I'm ready to move out of the past. I don't live there anymore! Sorry.

December 5

Lately, been reminiscing about my teenage years and the friends I had in those glorious moments of becoming what you believed was a man. I miss those guys, Aaron and Kevin; they were my best of friends anyone could have. I still talk to them, but we all went different ways a long, long time ago, but I'm happy they are doing well in life. I really am! You see, I'm also in love with being down and sort of sad or blue mood. I don't know why. I suspect that it is because I truly don't know the true joy that is given through my GOD. Although I recognize the joy he has graciously given, I am also familiar with the dark side of my emotions.

You see, I spent so much time getting high and drinking whiskey like Kool-Aid, and with my abundance narcotics, I've been numb to the very existence of my being. So, the transition to being somewhat sober is foreign to me. I don't know a sober life that well, so that dark, mysterious profile that I fit so well with is the norm for me, the sadness kind of makes me feel alive. The fucking irony. My life is stagnant as my childhood friends have moved forward in life. I face the epitome of my life of rebellion. I hope to write about my growing up and the friends that were so prevailing to me in those times.

December 9, 2015

I'm becoming unmotivated in several of my duties of mutant living. if mean, what the fuck does it take to have peace.? if know there is peace in the love of the Lord, but hey, man, it's also a battle between the spirit against the flesh. Dammit, man, it is a daily struggle. Last night got together with Chad and his cousin Terry; we call him lil' T. He is a great musician from whom I learned much from over the years. We rocked out like old times, but I was struggling to maintain my nerves due to my social anxiety that I suffer with, over the fact I'm a different person, not necessarily a good thing. I'm an introverted mutant today compared to a past Kebee that was confident and vigilant and, yeah, cocky. As if I was always in control. That's a problem when hanging out with old friends. There were very awkward moments that seemed to last long enough to expose the leftovers of KEBEE. I could hear them saying in my mind when they were on their ride home, "What a shame. He is a broken lil' man with no fire or life in him anymore." I tried to reminisce, but I just didn't harness that way of telling the stories as if you were watching a movie as describe in detail of whatever adventure I lived to tell. I don't have it anymore for them kind of stories, but let me tell you about my son Keaton, then you see a spark under my ass that threatens to burn down the house. But these old friends don't wanna hear about my eight-year old. They want dirty, nasty, cruel-natured and sexual endeavors of the stickman.

My paranoia keeps me prudent, and I think that it a good quality in my transformation. Kind of goes over the edge at moments that I believe my dog Cowboy also suffers from paranoia. I held on last night for as long as I could take it, so it was a step forward for mental being these days. GOD BLESS!!

December 16, 2015

You know, I really haven't gone back and read all that I written about. I absolutely, no doubt, know the main subject of this project is Keaton. I know it might be suspiciously lame and all, and no truth to my transformation. You see, I never claim to be perfect, even to this very date, but it is very simple; I was lost and searching through this worm hole we call life. I needed some kind of adventure in chaos daily, reaching for the pinnacle of existence and its arousing power. I never got enough, never! So, I would call out to God, "What, what, what, why, why, why?" Then, one day, he answered me. I didn't even know if he knew me. Well, my friends he did. He asked in the way GOD DOES! KEBEE, what do you want? And I'll give you what your heart desires, movie star, rich and famous, beautiful women, or an athlete, a mansion, new cars? And, without hesitation, I answered, "I want a son!" For the life of me, I do not understand why that came out my mouth. I never really pondered the possibility of ever having a child. It was never in my to-do list. Well, that's because my heart said it; my heart made the request. It had been a long time since my heart and my mind had connected to my heart. I honestly believed I had burnt those receptors clean out. That's what GOD ASKED! Tell me what your heart desires; truly, it was a son. I remembered that one evening taking a bath at Heather's, while she was in the bathroom putting on makeup. I suddenly became aware of a dream or vision that I had some time back, a day or a week prior. I can't recall the day I had the vision; I just profoundly understand that it was God that told me he has given me a seed, a good seed he says, while I'm sitting in a boat during a storm. I remember this to every detail, and I'm expressing it to Heather, and she really payed no mind to it. After all, it's me telling another crazy story like I do.

I decided not to go in to detail about me, and Katy and Chad's wild New Year's Day and the day after, only that it was now 2006, and me and Heather went off and on for the next ten months, as well as me and Katy; back and forth is what we did. I had love for both of them, but in the end of October I was with Katy and I was sure I was gonna spend the rest of my life with her. I totally handled that situation wrong, and it is what it is. Me and Katy couldn't get it together, well, I couldn't. Like I said in the beginning of the story, I knew a kid would be coming, and I thought it was Katy, but it was Heather, and I by no means was less excited and have not a twinkle of regret. These two women are both very respectable and beautiful, inside and out, and had no business keeping company with a rube and dope fiend outlaw. I truly loved and cherished my time with Katy, and she probably has no idea or clue of this love I speak of. She is very special to me. I guess it was not meant to be. Me and Heather moved in together, and I loved her more than she thought I did. That was our whole problem, and on top of me putting on the brakes to my lifestyle, which I'm still in a screeching slide, but wow, what can I say; Keaton came along in the hot melting heat of summer in 2007, and me and Heather only stayed together a couple months after he was born. I must say that was some hard times for me "mentally," but after a couple months later, I got it together enough to have Keaton as much as I wanted, and that is a whole lot. We spend every opportunity we get to be together in the eight years of his life, and two months after Keaton was born, Randy and Lexi had a baby, my beautiful little niece Lana, which is awesome knowing they would grow up with each other and be just as close as brother and sister. Everything was changing. These kids, including Randy and Lexi's first born Ashton, we were all a close nit lil' family, but it still was a struggle for me and Randy to get off the hustle way of life, but life was slowing down, and it made me a little dizzy, but I was maintaining. What happened three years later rocks me and my family and a community to its core.

CHAPTER 9
Breathe

December 19, 2015

You know, sometimes I feel like I'm on Jacob's ladder, but my own "Kebee ladder." Am I dying? Am I seeing my life flash in front of me as I slowly slide out of my fleshly worldly being? Is this a real life, or is it how life would have been? Well, I could have done better with my time. The best thing is the time with Keaton, and if I am on the deathbed holding on, it would be for that reason. Keaton, my total reason to hold on. I keep hearing the voices saying and whispering of angels along with the screaming of the demons, "Let go, just let go." What am I afraid of? I run the race up to now with a steady, consistent pace. I fight the good fight of faith. Let go, Kebee, let go. The stickman has been put to rest. I can't because I don't know how. I saw life come into this world, and I saw life taken out of it. So, I know, give me death! But not now; "I'm not finished. LORD,GIVE ME MORE TIME!" I breathe to know I'm alive. I know I have something to offer, and I will find the peace of mind. Yeah, yeah, I got something to offer. The best of my life has begun; I have to believe this. I'm ready to have a genuine smile from happiness and joy, instead of the usual smile through the relentless hurt. This is my battle daily but guess what. I'm not going to battle anymore. I give to my GOD and to my savior Jesus. Amen!

December 20, 2015

Eleven hundredth of a second, faster than a blink of an eye, that's how fast that you are here on Earth in the flesh, then in an instant in the presence of the Lord. You will not feel death or taste it. Let's just say I have seen it happen in front of me. God's time and our time is on a different scale. He is never early nor late, right on time, patience, patience, faith, faith, and more faith is the key. I just recently gained the understanding of faith, and it works. Ask through prayer and wait with belief, true to the heart belief. Ask once, no need to keep asking; he heard you the first time. If you continue to ask the same thing over and over then that means you have no faith in him or yourself. Wait on him! It is difficult for me, but I am trying.

January 2, 2016

Well, Christmas and New Year's came and went without any trouble. I have a longing in my heart that will not disappear. I really don't want it to go away. You see, in the year that changed many lives forever, 2010 started off with Randy calling me nine minutes away from the New Year. He asked me to go meet him and Lexi at their house, which was no longer in the apartment complex. They had a nice piece of land with a new mobile home close to the basin. Randy had just recently finished having a shop built for his bike and enough room to work on and turn wrenches on a bike. Well, I got the call and was in Lafayette. I immediately jump on my bike, which was a different bike than the Nighttrain, a Harley Nightster which was given to me by my older brother Mike. it was cool, orange and black and fast. Well, I made to their house in nine minutes. I swear; people say it is impossible, but I did it! Me and Randy stayed outside, and we were just bullshiting and thinking back and thinking towards our future. Randy is forever in my mind and heart, and I miss him beyond dearly. In eight months into 2010, August 19, 2010, I held Randy in my arms as he took his last breath, shot twice with a saw-offed shot gun at close range. The shooter was his childhood friend and about the closet person next to family in Randy's life. I'll talk more about that later, because it breaks my heart.

January 7, 2016

I'm sitting here thinking and reflecting on ideal moments of the stickman, and you know, I once said I have done nothing absolutely nothing to contribute to the world. I took advantage of our rights as a American in this USA, freedom, freedom that the real heroes and the legends of the military, the ones who gave their lives, their blood, sweat, and tears. I can't imagine being a young man, having to go out and kill, but these young men and women done it! Freedom is doing exactly what you wanna do without any fear in doing it. So, ask yourself, are you free? War will always be! Can't imagine the carnage these kids seen and done. Myself, I fucked around and never had to go to fight in a foreign land. I have fantastic respect for all serving and veterans, the real heroes. I'm a nobody, a fucking stickman. Man, I'm ashamed. Randy looked up to me, and I dropped the ball and brought him to a luring of evil way of life and glorified it. You know, a lot of people knew and loved Randy, but them people moved on as soon as he was lowered down into the earth, not me, not my family, not fucking me, not fucking me, not fucking me. I miss him, and I'm at a lost in my beautiful existence.

January 13, 2016

The main objective of my writings is the change that has occurred in the last eight years. The entropy of the stickman has slowly taken its course. It is a magnificent ride to nowhere that ultimately leads to me. You need to understand that Keaton's existence is key to my story in multiple ways. I, without a doubt, would absolutely, I can't stress this enough, the coward that shot and killed my baby brother Randy, needs to pray often more than normal. Pray that this slick, slimy, silver-tongue son of a bitch has not avenged his death! Why? Simple. "Keaton." I have a duty to be there always for my son and nieces and nephew.

So, thank the good Lord, you coward, that Keaton is in this world, because if he weren't, you would have suffered a swift grim-fated hurt and agony. First, I would have taken a spoon and scooped your eye balls out; maybe torture you for days on end!

January 14, 2016

Life is a score of lessons to be learned. If you haven't learned anything from your mistakes and misfortunes, then they will continue to keep you going in circles. I know this, never run out of cigarettes if you smoke like I do, don't get in cars with men who wear pinky rings and drive Cadillacs because you may end up riding in the trunk, humble yourself, treat all children as if they were your own, give more than you take, be yourself, get a Bible, and get a gun! Love your family, cry when needed, explore, treat women the way you want your sister and mother to be treated, keep things simple, don't fear change, don't build a house where you can pitch a tent. Just a few things to start a transition of life. I'm waiting in love and now in love with waiting. Let's go back and recap 2006. The inscription reads:

no farewell words were spoken, no time to say goodbye,
you were gone before we knew it only God knows why

{Randy's epitaph}

CHAPTER 10
The Transition

In the early to late 2006, I was out of control and probably close to death. I could smell my own demise, I tell you. Drinking and smoking, eating and snorting, literally breathing meth. The stickman was in his peak of existence. Me and Heather were off and on and so was the same for me and Katy. I was in a whirlwind and stuck in a ditch. The positive side of this situation is that I was aware of it. Some people don't know they are stuck in a ditch, poor mutants. I was barely hanging to a thread of reality. Then, in late November, Heather announced she was pregnant, and I was the father! I jumped and hollered and screamed with joy that I had not felt since a child when you wake up for Christmas morning. That was pretty much the end of me and Katy, and then, in December, Lexi announced that her and Randy were pregnant. That made so happy because our kids would grow up with each other and that would mean we would all spend good quality time with each other, "a family, a future of our family." Man, everything was changing, but it was not easy or instant. It was and still is a struggle, but you could see the change in me and Randy, although we did not completely cut all the stickman, outlaw ways. That's who we were and are, just not in the chaos of the lifestyle. So, the next few years were great. We were all living the American dream as they call it. Shit, I had become a suburban mutant. It is worth it; Keaton is my lifesaver, without any doubt. Although me and Heather only lasted two months after Keaton was born, but we have always remained close and civil for the proper raising of Keaton. I promised Keaton that I would always be there for him, and I have not let him down to this day. Randy was enjoying his family and working steady as a air conditioner repair guy. He was doing well. For myself, I was struggling mentally due to my outrageous partying in the past and my binges I was still indulging in, but it was from time to time and not every day and never when Keaton was with me.

I have to stay out of jail and stay alive and out of the mental hospital for the promise I made to my son. I love saying that, my son! From 2007 to late 2010, things were overall good and as close to normal as possible. I had a few meaningless relationships; most of my spare time is spent with Keaton, so that's where my full attention and love is, towards him. The stickman ways and the friends gradually faded out from my life. I and Randy, just kept a couple of important people in our circle. The ones that were trustworthy and loyal, that would keep us in the mix but from the sidelines. There were no more weed runs or any major drug distributing , but we knew who was running our old enterprise, and we would get cut in for a lot of action because of the connections we made over the years, but we weren't hands on anymore. I was cool with that. Life was good, until that Thursday night in August of 2010.

I can't go on much more about that dreadful night for several reasons that I will not disclose. I can say this, I'm off the wagon on most of this story from the beginning. I feel absolute shame. The next day or three days later, after drinking whiskey straight out the bottle, hoping for the answer at the bottom of it, all along smelling meth like an old love flame that has found me after all these years, but never during my time with Keaton. I don't expect at all to stay off the wagon indefinitely; it's just the only possible way to extract any of the stickman's endeavors. I'm focused on what is and what is to be "you dig?"

I don't ride motorcycles no longer and not in the pursuit of the female and her counter parts for myself or to sale for perverted suburban mutants.

I laugh at these guys, because if you see it from my perspective, only then will you realize what kind of brutal power and complete control that pussy has over men, and not to mention women as well. There, I said it. Forgive me, Lord, for the wretch I am with my carnal mind. I'm out that business altogether. I shit you not! after Randy's death, everything just didn't seem the same, and if I could have taken it for him, I would have, no doubt, but I was totally incapable of doing anything, and I feel like a failure, and it's my fault. I introduced both of them boys, Randy and the shooter. I won't mention his name because he don't deserve to be recognized other than the coward. I introduced them to a fucked-up way of life, where street credit and a reputation as a motherfucker that can take care of business, kind of straight shooter and loyal guy. What happened that night opened the eyes of a lot of people. Yeah, and now my little brother has two fatherless kids, a soulmate left alone, a twin sister without her baby brother, and my parents, me and Mike left here without him, just the memory of a great man. That's all any one can say!

I'm different these days, far from perfection, but different in a better Kebee. I want to make sure no one glorifies the way I lived and makes anyone think they can repeat my way. Stop, I say, stop, and get right, because you can't imitate my life; you can't mirror my life and think for one minute that you can survive the stickman way! You know, the most beautiful moment in my life happened when Heather called me and told me Keaton reaction after I went to his school for a lunch with a loved one.

Keaton told his mom Heather that when he saw that I was there, he almost cried. "But, Mom," he said, "I manned up!" I cried for two reason. as I cry writing this at this very moment. First is that's how much he loves me, that just showing up for a lunch; wow, that's heavy on my heart. When I was in school as a young boy, the last thing I wanted was my parents at my school. I would have been embarrassed for no particular reason. That's just how I felt, along with the other kids in agreement. We would tease kids if their mom or dad gave them a kiss goodbye while being dropped off at school and, God forbid, say I love you. lol Different world today. But, wow, that meant more to me. I know he loves me but wanting to cry for happiness to see me is heart-warming, and it's not like we don't see each other often, because we are together as much as possible, but the second is that he had to suck it up. That's the beginning of the end of the pure heart because of thinking having to be tough and not cry.

He didn't fall and hurt himself where that would be acceptable and you would hear "shake it off "; no, he wanted to cry for happiness! That's pure love from God that has been harnessed which will eventually turn in to a stickman kind of heart (hard). But I cry and say if you got to walk away and hide, "Cry, my lil' baby boy, cry, cry!"

January 24, 2016

I'm so angry, even angry at GOD himself. When I'm hurting, a switch in me goes to anger mode. I try to stay calm, but usually I end up in trouble, or the police make their prompt presence. What I'm getting at is the guilt I feel, the unconditional love I have for my family. The guilt is brought upon my niece and nephew, Randy's children, of which Lana doesn't remember her dad as Ashton does, but even ash don't have a great recollection of him, but he has some. So, when I'm doing all what I can do to be a great father, I tend to think of how Randy would be the same or even better. So, my heart hurts, and I cry often over this. I thank my lil' sis Angie, who watches them two plus her own, Bree, and then she watches Keaton at times also. She makes sure, and I do my part, but not as much as my parents and Angie that give the kids all the love they can, but in my mind, it still is not the same as them having their dad, but its damn close. This is what drives me to the edge, to the unreturnable line of what I almost cross. I mean I'm standing on the motherfucking line of going get revenge for Randy. I have keep reminding myself "the kids, Kebee." They don't need another fatherless kid and no uncle around rather in prison or buried, they lose. But I wanna just do it sometimes. I won't though, I won't! I will not pull his eyeballs out with a spoon and put them in my fucking pocket!

January 26, 2016

Enough of that shit! If weren't for Keaton and Ashton, Lana, and Bree, I would absolutely have taken care of the situation personally. I'm a sad, kinda dark person in general. I love that emotion. What a sick bastard I am. The kid brings a smile to my now heavier build, and my hair is not only receding, its retreating. I sort of lost my smile and my strut, but I have a relationship with God that is building. "Kebee, what you doing?" "I'm building," is my reply. No more wild nights with loose women; no more of a lot of the stickman. I'm just an aging has-been. The world is so different and has less morals than an average stickman adventure. Sad, sad, sad. There is another person that I come to realize that is a ray of vibrant sunshine in my transition to a suburban mutant, and her name is Nevaeh, and Nevaeh comes with a lil' boy that I see having no trouble of being around me and my family. This is something I hope for because I'm waiting in love and becoming in love with waiting. I am not sure she knows exactly how I feel. Maybe I'll tell her soon.

I can't not help to think about my hitchhiker friend Arthur. Over the years, I'm blind sighted with an epiphany of that is a word or an example in real time of what he shared with me. I am leaning on the thought more and more that he was and is one of my guardian angels. I want to foolheartedly believe this. What a strange journey we call life; what a strange kind of existence we are!

In closing

I end this story here. There are many untold stories of the stickman that will later be revealed.

I leave you with this; how could say you are good if you haven't known evil? AND how could you say you are evil if you have not known good?

The end.

One last thing as you put a label of who you think I am, I'm gonna tell this; I was working as a maintenance man, and as maintenance man, you need tools.

Well, I got an itching to buy this top of the line cordless drill. The price tag is a little over two hundred dollars. One day, I made my mind up to go and purchase this badass drill, and it was slightly raining out, and I notice a woman walking on the side of the road on my way to the local Home Depot. She looked familiar; she looked like an old girlfriend, very attractive, by the way. So, I go on to the Home Depot with thoughts of my times with my old fling. I go in down the aisle of drills, and I just stared at this drill with its giant price tag, and I grabbed it, and then I suddenly stop and returned it to its place on the shelf. I could not understand my change of heart. So, I'm walking out of the store, and at the exit, there is a foyer or patio area with swings for your outside cool afternoons and coffee morning times. There is the same young woman I saw walking, and sure enough, as we met eyes, it was her. I give her a smile, and she returned one to me. She said, "Kebee?" I replied yes, and how have you been, and why are you sitting here, and what are you reading? She tells me, "I'm reading the Bible but in French." That was odd, and of course, I ask why. "So the devil can't understand me," she said. She asked me to sit with her so we could catch up with each other. Before I sit with her, I ask if she were thirsty because I was, so I walk up to the Coke machine right across against the wall from the swings where we were, and just for a laugh, I walked up to the machine and hit the Coke

button and gave a swift kick to its side, and wow, two Cokes fell into the tray where you retrieve your beverage; no shit, two Cokes. I was a little shocked but quickly acted as I meant for it to happen. She looked at me and said, “Only fucking Kebee.” We both laughed for a moment, then I sat down with each of us drinking our free Coke.

After the norm of small talk, I again ask why she was walking and sitting there. She told a story of have been living with her grandmother, and they were at some differences, and it was raining out, so she thought that this would be a good place to blow off steam and get out the weather. She went on about some other struggles she was encountering, some I knew all too well personally. Time was passing by, and I was now late to be back at work, and then I understood why I didn’t buy that drill that has been on my mind for weeks. I tell her to come with me. She reluctantly agreed, and I assured her to trust me. We got in my truck and headed to the store on the corner. I told her I would be right back, and she asked for one of my Marlboros, and I told her yes as I was walking into the store. I come out with a bag full of snacks and three packs of smokes and some drinks, also. I get in, and she thanked, me but she had nowhere to go at the moment. I headed towards a decent hotel and went in and rented a room for two days but told the clerk not to tell me where or the number of the room, that a young woman would be coming in for those details. As soon as I leave, I went to the truck. She looked at me with a totally perplexed look, as if I was there to have sex with her. Then I explained that she needed to go inside; there was a two-day room paid in full for her, and I hope things turn out good for her and shit like that. She asked if I were going to get down and hang out. I told her that I will not even see which direction she walked toward. Not to give me any clue where the room could be. She hugged me, and as she walking into the lobby doors, I yelled, “Check in the drawer next to the bed and read it. The devil I’m sure is bilingual.” Yeah, that was worth not having a drill.